A HAND TO HOLD

Written by Alexander Grant
Illustrated by Bruce Grant

Alexander Grant
A Hand to Hold
Printed in the United States of America
ahandtoholdbook@gmail.com

ISBN 978-1-54398-563-4

Writer's Bio

Alexander Grant was raised by his artist parents in Austin, Texas. He set off on his own journey - first to Boston where he received his BA in Journalism - before finally landing in Los Angeles. Writing since childhood, he is influenced by his surroundings and the people around him. *A Hand To Hold* was inspired by his love for animals and a lifelong goal to work in collaboration with his father, Bruce. It is a story of love as seen through the eyes of a young otter pup. This is Alexander's first children's book.

Instagram: ahandtoholdbook

Illustrator's Bio

Bruce Grant is an illustrator and graphic designer living in Austin, Texas. Originally from Houston, he attended Texas State University where he received his BFA degree. With these watercolor illustrations in *A Hand to Hold*, he wanted the images to capture the attention of young readers through a vibrant, happy color palette while also being realistic.

Instagram: bgrantaustin

Under the bright blue sky at the edge of the sea,

Lives Sammy C. Otter as happy as can be.

He and his parents love to splash and swim;

Their days filled with fun right up to the brim.

In order to stay close they've perfected their craft.

They hold hands while sleeping to form a little fur raft.

Sammy longs for a partner, like Mama has Dad;
Someone to pull close through good times and bad.

One day he decides to do something bold!
He sets off to find his own hand to hold.

Just down the coast
perched up on a rock,
Sits a big grey goose away
from her flock.

Slowly but surely, he crawls over the sand,

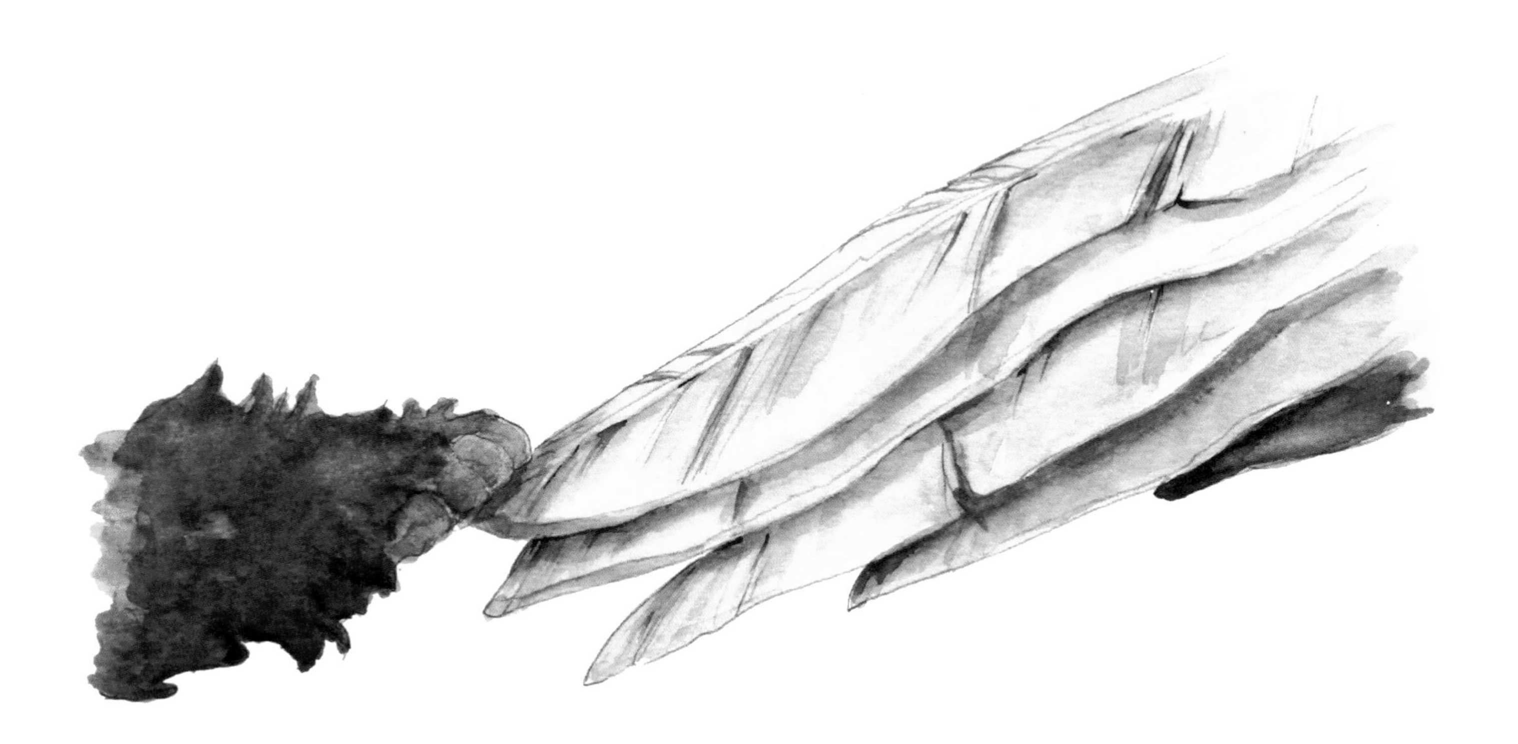

Gently grabbing her wing with his tiny left hand.

Almost at once, Sammy loosens his clutch.
The feathers, they tickle a little too much!

He doesn't get sad as the geese fly away.
Instead he heads out to swim in the bay.

Sammy dives down below to fulfill his wish.

There he stumbles upon a small school of fish.

All seems to be fine they make a good pair...
Until Sammy needs to come up for fresh air.

Try as he might, and he's one stubborn pup,

Sammy can't seem to convince
the fish to come up!

The sun is still shining as he heads toward the shore.
But all of this swimming is making him sore.

Just up ahead in the shade of a tree,
The sight of a turtle fills Sammy with glee!

Her hand doesn't tickle, nor is it too wet.
He's sure that this hand is the very best yet!

Except there's one thing that does not go so well;

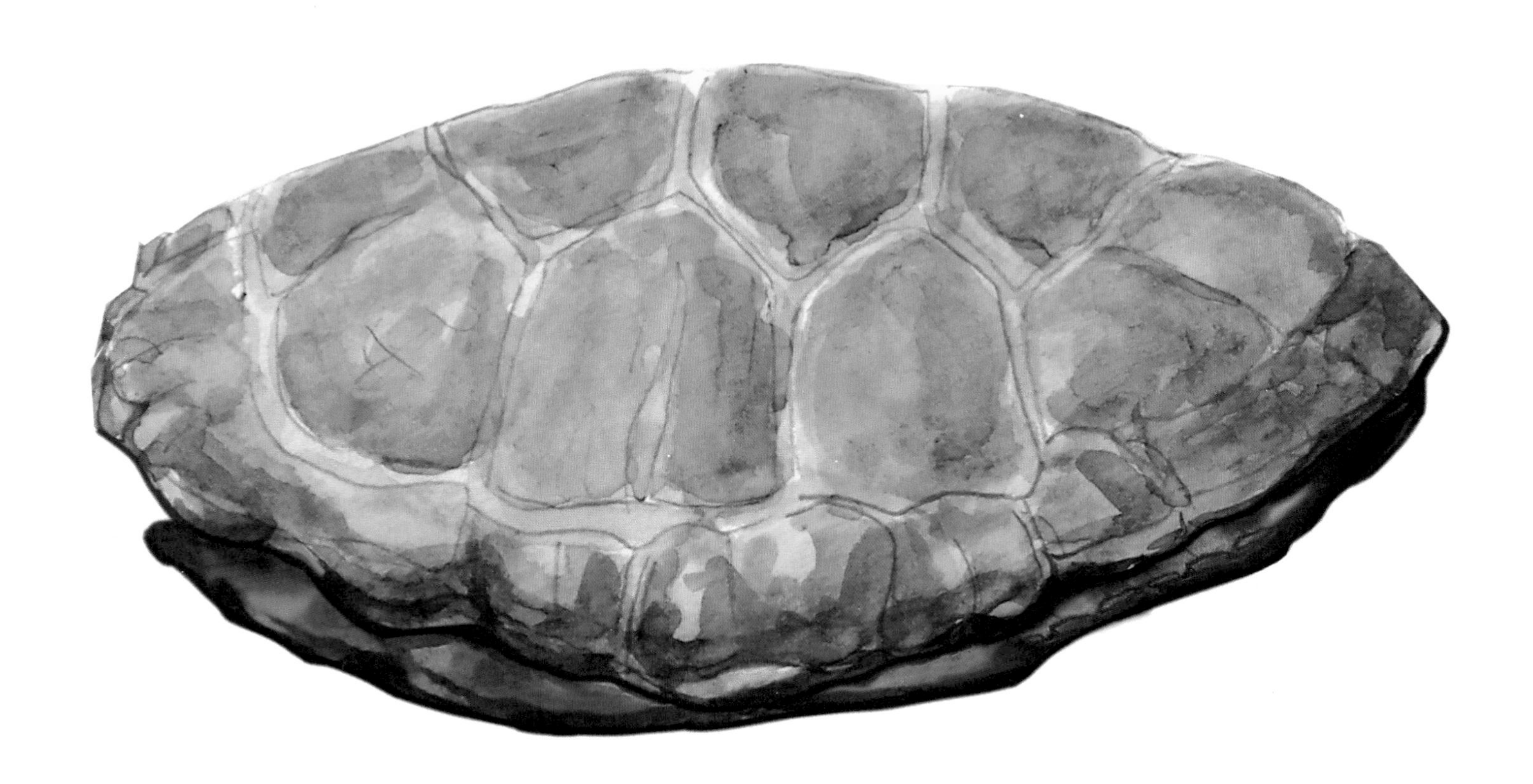

When turtles are sleeping they crawl inside their shell.

Sammy turns toward home - the sun starts to go down.
He can't keep his smile from becoming a frown.

He reaches the cove worn out from his trip.
Quietly, something brushes against his hip.

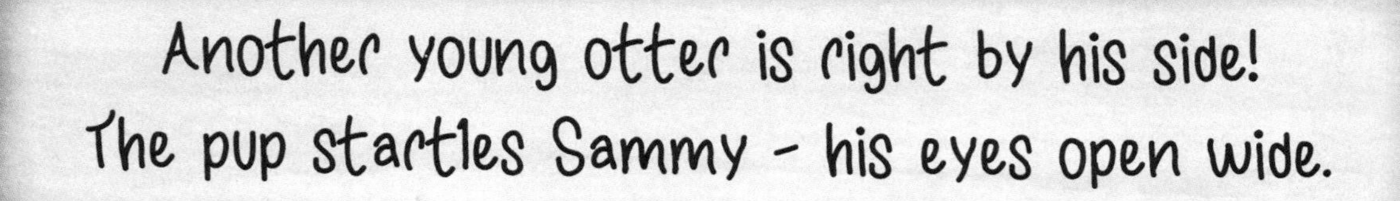
Another young otter is right by his side!
The pup startles Sammy - his eyes open wide.

Their hands fit together like two parts of one puzzle.
Sammy is happy to have someone to nuzzle!

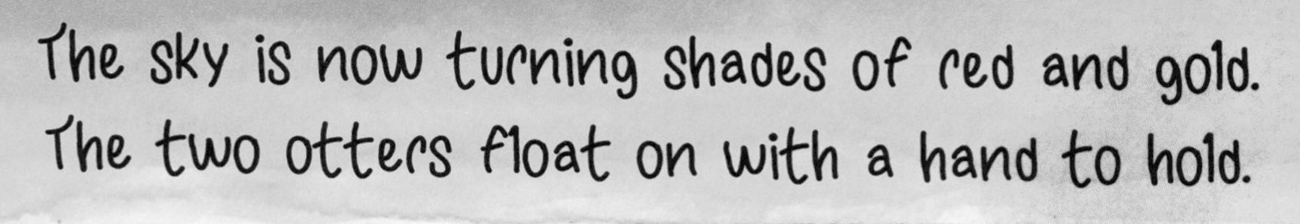

The sky is now turning shades of red and gold.
The two otters float on with a hand to hold.